MW00427279

RETURNING TO HER LEGENDARY SHORT STORIES, Pulitzer Prize and National Book Award finalist Joy Williams offers a much-anticipated follow-up to *Ninety-Nine Stories of God*, which *The New York Times Book Review* called a "treasure trove of bafflements and tiny masterpieces." *Concerning the Future of Souls* balances the extraordinary and the humble, the bizarre and the beatific, as Azrael—transporter of souls and the most troubled and thoughtful of the angels—confronts the holy impossibility of his task, his uneasy relationship with Death, and his friendship with the Devil.

Over the course of these ninety-nine illuminations, a collection of connected and disparate beings—ranging from ordinary folk to grand, known figures such as Jung, Nietzsche, Pythagoras, Bach, and Rilke; to mountains, oceans, dogs, birds, whales, horses, butterflies, a sixty-year-old tortoise, and a chimp named Washoe—experience the varying fate of the soul as each encounters the darkness of transcendence in this era of extinction. A brilliant crash course in philosophy, religion, literature, and culture, *Concerning the Future of Souls* is an absolution and an indictment, sorrowful and ecstatic. Williams will leave you wonderstruck, pondering the morality of being mortal.

Concerning the Future *of* SOULS

99 Stories of Azrael

JOY WILLIAMS

TIN HOUSE / PORTLAND, OREGON

This is a work of fiction. All of the characters, organizations, and events portrayed in this novel are either products of the author's imagination or are used fictitiously.

First US Edition 2024
Printed in the United States of America

Manufacturing by Versa Press
Interior design by Beth Steidle

Library of Congress Cataloging-in-Publication Data

Names: Williams, Joy, 1944– author.
Title: Concerning the future of souls : 99 Stories of Azrael / Joy Williams.
Description: Portland, Oregon : Tin House, 2024.
Identifiers: LCCN 2024003474 | ISBN 9781959030591 (hardcover) | ISBN 9781959030652 (ebook)
Subjects: LCSH: Soul—Fiction. | LCGFT: Fantasy fiction. | Short stories.
Classification: LCC PS3573.I4496 C66 2024 | DDC 813/.54—dc23/eng/20240205
LC record available at https://lccn.loc.gov/2024003474

Tin House
2617 NW Thurman Street, Portland, OR 97210
www.tinhouse.com

DISTRIBUTED BY W. W. NORTON & COMPANY

1 2 3 4 5 6 7 8 9 0

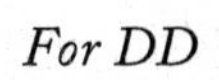

CONTENTS

Concerning the Future *of* SOULS

1

THEY LIVED IN NEW YORK CITY IN AN APARTment overlooking a park. It was the park, his parents said. You were always supposed to say *the* park. His father was sick. He began being sick a year before when he had laryngitis. His father had been interested in the sickness for awhile but now he was not. His mother had never wanted to understand it and did not want to learn anything about the machines his father required. This was not because she didn't love his father, he was told. People who knew the machines and how to care for them came in every day but they did not spend the night. His father spoke little to his mother but he would talk to him in his strange new voice. He did not like it. He did not like trying to talk to his father about school or soccer or the doorman's puppy which he had only seen pictures of anyway.

Every few weeks they would leave the city and visit his grandmother who lived with her brothers in a large house by the ocean. You could not see the ocean except for a tiny part of it and even that sometimes disappeared. Everyone in the house was old—or *elderly* was a word he had learned—and there were no children anywhere. Still, he did not mind these visits, he was somewhat hypnotized by them in fact.

They didn't seem to know each other well though they must have known each other better than anyone else. They would make popcorn for him in a pot on the stove and not the microwave. They didn't have a microwave. His mother had confided in him once that his father's family were rich oddballs and that their home was full of kitsch.

"Kitsch," his mother had explained, "isn't in itself beautiful but instead elicits its emotion from the beauty it depicts. Like that black ceramic panther in the bookcase."

"I love that panther," he said.

"Of course you don't love it," his mother said.

He did and one of his great uncles had given it to him but he broke it playing with the necklace it wore and he did not cry.

They showed him a photograph of his father as a boy. When he was the same age you are, they told him. His father's eyes were dark, even disbelieving. He wanted to ask what he had been looking at, though he did not, because he didn't believe it either.

KITSCH

2

WHAT IS YOUR NAME?

Alph.

Ralph?

Alph.

How do you spell that?

A. L. P. H. as in: *Alph the sacred river ran through caverns measureless to man down to a sunless sea.*

I don't think you're right for this position.

HUMAN RESOURCES

3

HE HAD FOUR THOUSAND WINGS. THIS was simply a fact. The feathers of each wing—innumerable. As they should be. The wings sheltered the souls so they could not be viewed in transit. This too was correct. He also had a thousand eyes but not, as has been rumored, four heads. Azrael was spectacularly made and looked nothing like Jesus as was so tirelessly depicted though in truth the Nazarene was not at all as rendered either. Jesus and Azrael were not well acquainted. They traveled in different circles. Jesus was surprisingly unfamiliar with death other than his own.

The birds of the air were terrified of Azrael. His murmurs of assurance were incomprehensible to them. Their bones were hollow and filled with air. The sweetest air. Wasn't that enough?

IN LOVELY BLUE . . .
AROUND WHICH LIES MOST
LOVING BLUE . . .

*Hölderlin

4

THE DEVIL WAS ONCE CALLED SON OF THE Morning. He was the Morning Star.

Now he was a sop, a concession, an afterthought . . .

But this was just the inner voice talking, the still small voice, that little piece of God caught inside him like a fish bone, trying to make him feel bad. This was just God, who hadn't gotten over him and never would. He threw him out of heaven so he could reside on earth, what kind of reasoning was that? God had let jealousy overcome Him. Pique! He must have blanked out. And in the Devil's estimation, He had never blanked on again. He had doubled down in the loving-the-little-human-children department at the expense of everything else. It was all so credulous and sentimental and people just lapped it up. Such love could not be overjustified. The situation was unsustainable.

The Devil clawed a bit at the site of the lodged fish bone which was hardly a torment but more than an irritation. His heart beat on unperturbed. He had a good strong heart still, one that had never given him any trouble.

5

A DREAMER IS DREAMING.

Two young men visit him. They are thin and blond. They wear jeans and a somewhat foreign looking blousy garment.

They are here, they tell him.

They lead him into a large arena with clean sawdust on the floor. It is pleasantly bright but he's unsure as to where the light is coming from. The windows that he notices are covered with black cloth or paper.

There they are, they tell him.

Two elephants stand in one corner, their trunks entwined. His instinct is to speak, to ask a question but then he feels it is better to be quiet. He is quiet.

Touch them, one of the angels says.

He makes his way toward the elephants. He walks and walks. The light never wavers though surely darkness has fallen by now.

OPPORTUNITY

6

ONE OF THE MOST IMPORTANT PHILOSOPHER theologians of Western Europe in the high Middle Ages was the Franciscan John Duns Scotus. He wrote on grammar, logic, and metaphysics and was praised for the nuance and complexity of his thought. Two of his most dazzling and beautiful concepts concerned *Haecceity* and the *Univocity of Being*. Haecceity is the "thisness" of every thing, that quality in all which is individualizing, particular. The Univocity of Being is the argument that we all are one in the oneness of God. All life—water, trees, animals—participate in the same Being and that Being is holy.

Certain renditions of Scotus show him wearing a snug vaguely conical hat and it might be more than legend that he believed this assisted in the retention of metaphysical wisdom. His Franciscan followers, the Dunsmen, wore headgear that somewhat exaggerated the conical shape. By the 16th century the ideas of Renaissance humanism prevailed in European thought with its emphasis on the self and the centrality of the human in the cosmos. The philosophy of Scotus was mocked. Duns (the simple village of his birth in Scotland) became a word of scorn and dunce a contemptuous term for someone dabbling in sophistry and incapable of true scholarship. The Dunsmen's telltale hats were depicted by the enemies of Scotus' thought as more and more preposterous and elongated, a witch or wizard's adornment. It was considered quite the opportunity for mirth, the idea of Univocity.

DUNCE

7

PYRRHULOXIAS NEST EARLY AMONG THE THORNS, building neatly of twigs, coarse grasses and fine fibers for lining. If you approach too near they voice a worried little purring "cheek cheek" full of plaintive friendliness. No one can hear that sound and remain unmoved.

PLEA

**Birds of the Southwestern Desert*
Gusse Thomas Smith

8

SHE WAS LYING ON SOFT SHEETS IN AN OLD motel on the beach. The day was sunny and fresh with a clean sea breeze. It was the past, but she was immersed in it in the present. It was wonderful. She didn't mind in the slightest that her friends weren't there. But then she started thinking about whales and grew sad. There were no whales here, the waters were too warm and shallow, but there were sharks. These were killed whenever seen. By the pool there was a red Coca-Cola machine with an endless supply of cold Cokes. In the room, above the bed, was a print of *Foxes and Geese* by

Johann Heinrich the Elder Tischbein. She'd had to look it up, what it was. A peculiar choice for an old beach motel. Someone here was being a little eccentric, she thought. They were about to tear the place down any minute and they had actually. She had come here with friends or, in any case, a number of people she knew, but now she was alone, thinking about whales, worrying about them. They were in terrible danger. She couldn't grasp the enormity of the whale, the extraordinariness of their lives. Her own life had been quite unmysterious, but a whale's life in the ocean! Amazing. *Sound never ceases* in the water. She'd learned that in school and it stuck. Funny, certain things, the way they do after years and years. The depths were not silent at all. There was always sound—ticking and groaning and singing and shattering and the whales heard and comprehended it all. Whales did no harm and were possessors of the ocean's meaning. But they were being slaughtered. Oh she didn't want to be thinking this. What if this were the last thing she'd be given to think?

ASYLUM

In vain do they flee. No
longer have they any asylum
but in nothingness.

* Bernard Germain de Lacépède
The Natural History of the Cetaceans

9

THIS IMAGE IS NO
LONGER AVAILABLE

10

ON SEPTEMBER 12, 2021, FOURTEEN HUNDRED dolphins in dozens of family pods were killed in the Faroe Islands. They'd been herded by motorboats, jet skis and all manner of personal watercraft into a bay to be slaughtered on the beach. This was not commercial whaling, this was a community event, a cherished custom that rather got out of hand. Six times more dolphins were killed in a single day than an entire year. Usually it's pilot whales who are tapped for this free food but a large number of dolphin were sighted by some mariner on September 12 and the community went delirious with excitement. As part of this cherished tradition there are people on shore poised to dispatch the gifts of the sea with an implement called a spinal lance which is said to reduce killing time to One—well possibly two—second(s) but there weren't enough butchers on the beach—it's always more fun to be on the boats—and so very many desperate and terrified and dying mammals that the One (possibly two) second refinement of the spinal lance couldn't be humanely applied.

The intoxicating orgy of killing will have to serve as its own reward for no one can really say how much of the flesh was processed and distributed to grateful Faroe Islanders. Or what was done with the carcasses of the families. There might be a tradition of respectful disposal though this is not likely. The remains were probably just dumped into the blood black sea.

SENTIENCE

11

Why not?

MAY THE JUDGMENT NOT BE
TOO HEAVY UPON US

*T.S. Eliot

12

SOME THOUGHT THAT AZRAEL WAS THE angel God had sent to earth to bring back the dust from which he would make a human. Azrael did not believe he was the one so chosen. Surely he would have remembered such a strange journey! Lost in the fogs of storytelling now—the identity of the one who delivered to God the fateful dust.

Anything else? the angel, whoever he was, might well have asked.

No, God said. Just dust.

Everyone assumed that He knew what he was going to do with it. One of God's favorite elements was water so that would undoubtedly be involved in turning dust into whatever He had in mind, but what else might be added the angels had not a clue. Maybe nothing. The Divine was rumored to like working with very little.

. . . WHO ARE WE? WE ARE ALL MADE OF MUD . . . WE ARE FULL OF IT, WE ARE NOTHING BUT MUD.

*John Calvin
Dieu

13

THE DEVIL'S FAVORITE PARABLE CONCERNED the man who came to the marriage feast for the king's son but was not dressed properly and was thrown out. In general he preferred knowledge vs. understanding teachings and this one, where the pretender was cast weeping into the outer dark, was one of the best.

MATTHEW

22:2–14

14

HE BROUGHT HER A BUNCH OF SUNFLOWERS and a package of discounted hot cross buns for that day had passed. She found a jar that contained a few pickles, dumped them out and stuffed the flowers in. The effect managed to be splendid. She allowed the buns a plate.

He spoke about his despair.

"No, really," he said.

"If you take your life . . ." she began.

He laughed. "It sounds like marriage."

"It is a marriage," she said. "Like no other."

She looked at him stubbornly and he realized she'd been drinking. He stuffed a stale bun in his mouth. "Do you have any whiskey to go with this?" he asked.

She brought out a bottle of whiskey and they drank and ate the Easter buns.

WYRD

15

IN THE BEGINNING HE WANTED TO WRITE poetry because he had fallen in love with words. What the words stood for was of secondary importance. "I tumbled for words at once," he said. His poems can be enjoyed without understanding them in the slightest. His later work tended to be a bit showy however. He adored drinking. His wife Caitlin adored drinking as well and once remarked that the bar was their altar. Sometimes he would get the shakes or what he called the horrors when abstractions—triangles, squares, circles and cones—would descend upon him. Earlier in the night that he fell into a coma, he claimed that he had drunk eighteen whiskeys at his favorite New York tavern but the bartender said this was an exaggeration and he had only drunk eight. The cause of his death at thirty-nine was acute alcoholic encephalopathy with pneumonia and emphysema contributing. His gravemarker is nothing fancy.

His name is inscribed, followed by, R.I.P.

DYLAN THOMAS SPOKE NO WELSH

16

WHEN AZRAEL WAS AN INFANT HIS SIRE would sing *Ghost Riders in the Sky* to him at bedtime. His sire had a beautiful singing voice and Azrael could thrillingly picture the Devil's cattle with red and blazing eyes and hooves of steel stampeding across the heavens with the weary cowboys damned to pursue them for all eternity. These were cowboys who had lived an ungodly life and had never changed their ways when they'd been given multiple opportunities to do so. Azrael summoned up his courage and asked the Devil once if his stupendous and tireless herd were entirely red (as he had always imagined) and what did *yippie i oh yippie i ay* mean anyway? but the Devil was in one of his moods and just ignored him.

THE DEVIL'S HERD

17

ONE OF THE TRIPS SHE'D ALWAYS WANTED TO take—she didn't understand why exactly—was to Australia. She intended to experience the interior, not the coast. She wanted to climb the red Uluru. She found the surround ghastly—the tour buses, the viewing areas, the crowds and suppers of barbequed emu and kangaroo, the dreadful wine. Still, she felt fortunate that she'd been able to climb Uluru because the aborigines—whom she found interesting though it was difficult to know much about them—had been considering closing the sacred prominence to visitors. This was for the usual reasons—the littering, defecating, and engaging in sex on the trail, as well as knocking off fragments of the half-billion-year-old stone for keepsakes. She was glad she had climbed the red Uluru and survived the savagely vertical descent because the Aṉangu people did close the climb. Tourists co-operated with this decision for the most part, some even returning the bits of rock they'd carried off. The Aṉangu received boxes and boxes of rocks from everywhere, some with notes enclosed. What the fate of these fragments would be was a good question—surely they could no longer be considered part of the aggregate of reverence considering where they'd been. As for her own memento, she'd misplaced it almost immediately.

ULURU

18

I DIDN'T CRY OUT AS I PLUNGED THROUGH the darkness. I didn't know any better. Too busy thinking to myself, *This is how it is, this is how it is, how it is* . . . accustoming myself to what it seemed life brings, what life is. Spinning, tumbling, a breathless rush, terror, exhilaration and wonder, wondering is this it, am I doing it right.

CHUTE

*John Edgar Wideman
Newborn Thrown in
Trash and Dies.

19

THE NUMBER OF SOULS ARE FIXED. EACH birth is not the creation of a soul but the completion of the transmigration from one body to another. There is no such thing as a new soul. The souls made no sound as Azrael transported them. Never had one attempted to engage him in thought. The journey was made in perfect silence. They seemed wonderstruck.

I WAS GLAD TO . . .
BE HELD, WHETHER DEAD OR
UNBORN, I DID NOT CARE.

*Ted Hughes

20

HE HADN'T FELT WELL WHEN HE WOKE THAT morning but this was the case almost every morning. He would feel uneasy, even ashamed. He had been somewhere, he knew not where and had been brought back. It was incomprehensible. He grew calmer as the day progressed. Now it was almost evening and he was in his little garden with his dog and a glass of scotch. The dog accepted an ice cube as was customary. There was a thicket in the corner and the dog barked at it briefly like he always did. He did not like it. The man sipped his scotch and looked about them, for the moment, content. He thought of the story of the two monks sitting in a garden much like this one. After a long and pleasant silence, one of them broke into loud laughter. He pointed across the lawn and said, "They call that a tree," whereupon the other monk began to laugh as well.

The old man chuckled recalling this and gazing down at his dear dog said, "You're going to like this shampoo, it gets rid of flicks and teas." He regretted the words as soon as they left his mouth knowing with violent assurance that it wasn't at all what he ultimately would have wanted to say.

THICKET

21

TITUS ACCESSED 911 AND THE PERSON WHO answered said he was talking too fast, that he was incoherent. Then the person said, "I'm going to hang up now. I can't understand a word you're saying. You sound like a dog barking. Do you know your location? Call back when you're calmer."

EMERGENCY

22

TELL ME, THE DEVIL SAID, WHAT IS THE VERY worst thing that has happened to you?

Why? Azrael said. Then he parried. What is the very worst thing that ever happened to *you*?

He was aware this was not clever but he knew the Devil only wanted to talk about himself anyway.

The fall, of course, the Devil said. My defining moment. He added, It's been depicted many times. Of all the paintings, drawings and such, my favorite is by Gustave Doré. It shows me mid-careen as I descend to earth. Paul Gustave Louis Christophe Doré. He chose to be known as Gustave.

Azrael said, The name means "glorious guest." It's a rather popular name.

Fine artist, the Devil said. Dramatic. Excellent command of the line.

I've seen that portrait of you, Azrael said. You have it framed.

To my knowledge I have never invited you into my chambers, the Devil said loftily.

He'd always been vain. He'd been told it was one of his biggest problems.

HIS FAVORITE PICTURE

23

WHEN SHE WAS TEN SHE PLANTED A CHERRY tree for her mother's birthday. It was watered too heavily and died the following year. When she was twenty she planted a palm. Someone informed her that palms were not trees at all which she considered debatable.

When she was thirty she planted a grapefruit tree and wished she had planted it ten years before. It sickened when they had to hook up to a public sewer and the leach field dried. When she was forty she planted a copper beech. The town had taken down two mature ones to expand the hospital parking lot after the facility had been voted best rural hospital in the state two years in a row. It was only a slip of a gesture she knew, her copper beech. When she was fifty she planted an oak, just a good sturdy oak but she placed it too close to the electric lines and with increase in broadband demand it was sheared and lopped to an unsurvivable degree. When she was sixty she sentimentally planted a cherry tree once more. When she was seventy she planted a mulberry tree over the objection of her neighbors who found the berries attracted undesirable wildlife. When she was eighty she planted a hawthorn tree and was amused when the beautiful blossoms smelled rank rather than fragrant. She found amusing too, and this she would say to anyone inclined to listen, that though the Buddha was certainly no fool he had certainly overestimated our abilities to be responsible by a great deal.

8

24

THOMAS MERTON'S HOME ABBEY AT THE Gethsemeni's monastery in Trappist, Kentucky was dear to him but he increasingly bemoaned the lack of solitude there. There were so many visitors—a gift shop sold fudge and fruitcake—and there was the noise of the hunters' guns in the surrounding hills. America's most famous monk needed fresh spiritual challenges. In 1968 he flew to Asia "with a great sense of destiny" to explore the sacredness of other beliefs. He thrilled to the great stupas at Polonnaruwa in Sri Lanka. He was less enthused about Kanchenjunga, the mountain which rises to more than 28,000 feet and is known as the Sleeping Buddha. Merton tired of Kanchenjunga almost instantly, expressing annoyance "at its big crude blush in the sunrise" and noting in his diary, "When you begin each day by describing the look of the same mountain you were living in the grip of delusion." Later he relented a bit, reasoning, "But why get mad at a mountain?"

Merton believed—in the manner of St. Benedict—that a monk's most important vow was the commitment to total inner transformation, to become a completely new being.

Near the end of his planned Asian pilgrimage he gave a talk at an international conference on monasticism in Bangkok. Afterward he retired to his room, took a shower, and walked across the tiled floor to turn on a large standing fan. He was found some hours later, on his back with the fan running and lying across his chest. That Death would seek him out by means of a malfunctioning appliance seems preposterous but one shouldn't make too much of it.

THE FAN

25

LAKE BAIKAL IN SIBERIA IS A VAST ANCIENT lake, the deepest in the world. Near its shores are cemeteries which date back 7000 years to the Neolithic period, the end of what is referred to as the Stone Age. Numerous graves have been found containing dogs, indicating that some animals were considered unique beings deserving of ritual burial after death. Several graves have been found harboring the remains of wolves, and there is none more extraordinary than that of the Wolf of Baikal or Lokomotiv, a slangy term for the site unearthed by the construction of the Trans-Siberian Railway. This large, fully articulated canid was lying on its left side with its head to the south. Positioned between its flexed front legs was the cranium and mandible of an adult male human. A line of ocher in the shape of an oval extended outward from the wolf's front limbs. Paleontologists consider this most intriguing, even provocative, for the wolf's positioning suggests that he is intended to accompany and protect a human beyond the gates of absence and death. Long before the birth of the gods, someone clearly hoped that both these beings would be together always.

SOMEONE

26

HE PEERED INTO THE FREEZER. THERE SHOULD be one last portion of integrity raised beef in there. There were many people—most of them in fact—who didn't care much about the integrity of their food overmuch but he was not one of them. But there was nothing. No remnant of frolicsome calf raised to prime by loving kindergarteners, petted a hundred times a day by tiny hands, fed flowers and clover, surrounded by her most loyal and affectionate and trusted of caregivers, the ones who had named her and taught her to know that name was hers. No Tunnel of Death, no blood-slick and reeking duckboards. No inept stickers or angry leggers, no prodders or stunners. No knocking gun going *kachunk kachunk kachunk*. Just a last embrace in a lush and sunny field and the sound of little children's piping voices. Not a whiff of terror or foreboding in the air for her.

But the last of Hemera, raised by Mrs. Ricky Hormel's advanced preschool class of Hopewell, New Jersey, was not in the freezer. He must have finished it off some time ago and just forgotten.

HEMERA

27

DEEP BLUE, WHO APPEARED AS TWO CABINET towers three and a half feet tall, was the computer who beat the Russian grandmaster Garry Kasparov at chess back in the old 90s. It was then retired from programming (disassembled) and split up so it could reside in two museums at once. Deep Blue knew nothing but chess, it could only respond to moves in chess. Even its finest hour could not hold a candle to modern large language models comprised of billions of parameters that can generate human-like responses to questions not only in language but in images. Except with computers one does not ask questions but provides "prompts." For example, when the Google consultant James Manyika prompted one of the large language models with "Is the Turing Test a reasonable criteria for the achievement of general AI?" he received a cagey, multifaceted, somewhat indignant reply. (The term *artificial intelligence* isn't used much anymore, computers probably find it inexact . . .)

But say your prompt was, "What does the face of God look like?" you might not get a response. The large language model might well give you the equivalent of a blank stare which it's also capable of doing.

EVERYTHING PASSES AWAY EXCEPT HIS FACE . . . NOTHING OTHER THAN HIM HAS BEING AND THEREFORE HAS TO PASS AWAY SO THAT HIS FACE REMAINS. THERE IS NOTHING EXCEPT HIS FACE.

* The Quran

28

AZRAEL WAS IN THE VANISHED FOREST, AMIDST the smoldering stumps. The silence here really was as fearsome as the grave's. The sky seemed lifeless as well, a monstrously staring eye. Rain was falling hesitantly and sliding off the soil as if it were striking wax. More and more Azrael was arriving too late for the world. The logging had taken place months ago and the great trees had long since gone through—what was it called—the *processing sequence.* The forest had been a living being and now it was not. Azrael felt a little sick. He was still more or less on time with humans but was finding it harder and harder to keep up with everyone else. Death was the dark crude brother, he was the shining inspiriting one. His duties had always been performed gracefully and he was appreciated for his punctuality and beautiful manners. But how could the immensity of the earth and all her other children be assisted to insure their souls' regeneration? His methods were being disrupted by the sheer precipitous magnitude of it all.

HE'LL COME TO YOUR HOUSE
AND HE WON'T STAY LONG
YOU'LL LOOK AT THE BED AND
YOUR MOTHER WILL BE GONE

*the Reverend Gary Davis

29

SHE COULD PICTURE HIM AS ONE OF THOSE saints of legend, perishing in the desert, the animals he had so tenderly preached to digging his grave with their great claws.

THE STRANGE MAN'S BURIAL

30

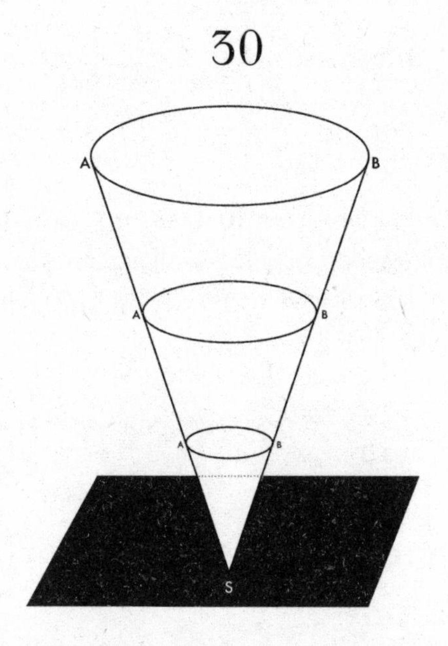

THE PHILOSOPHER HENRI BERGSON'S CONE OF Memory is famous but it's not as famous as it used to be.

THE PAST IS NOT DEPENDENT
UPON THE PRESENT FOR ITS EXISTENCE.

31

AZRAEL HAD READ A GREAT DEAL OF POETRY. So much so that he had to entrust his wings and eyes to remember it all. He was fond of Hopkins of course. That "Windhover"! The young man lived in an almost perpetual state of spiritual desperation and depression but he said No to it. No. No. No. Or sometimes. Many times he was overcome with a sense of failure and horror. He liked to draw trees and waves but wasn't as good at this as his brother Arthur. He wrote about them however in an extraordinary unsurpassable way.

This morning Azrael is thinking about that row of poplar trees on a meadow's river bank. Hopkins wrote:

All felled, felled, are all felled

Not spared, not one

and he compares the land of which they were a part to a sleek and seeing eye which by a slice, a nick becomes no eye at all. The trees have become unselved. Their home of earth and sky unselved as well.

Azrael shudders, rousing his feathers. If one of their eyes were nicked, they would all come to grief surely.

BINSEY POPLARS

32

THAT WAS A CLOSE CALL, SHE THOUGHT.

The fire truck had just blown through the red light. She definitely had the green but the car in front of her didn't move. She was dumbfounded at first but then, honking the horn indignantly, she swerved around the fool and into and through the intersection as the ridiculous red engine passed behind her.

The truck had come out of nowhere. Literally nowhere, she thought.

She was going home after dropping the dogs off at the kennel. She would only be home for a few hours before she had to leave again and drive in *the opposite direction* to the airport. It was so annoying because she had dropped the dogs off the day before and gone home for a few hours and driven to the airport only to discover that she had the date wrong, it was the next day, this day, she was supposed to leave. She'd collected the dogs because she didn't like to be away from them longer than necessary and then had to return them there just a few moments ago which bewildered them.

Now she thought she wouldn't even bother going home but would go directly to the airport. She was quite rattled having gotten the days wrong and just wanted to be on her way and get this trip over with. She would drive to the airport and have a few glasses of wine and a sandwich and maybe buy a magazine and wait for the goddamn plane. She was close, very close, when she recalled that the terminal was closed between midnight and four. Locked up tight. She'd have to wait outside in the car and that's what she would do. She was upset with herself, she felt beside herself really.

THIS VAST TERMINAL
HAS BEEN ERECTED TO
EXAMINE SOULS.

*Don DeLillo
The Names

33

THE ELYSIAN FIELDS SHOULD NOT BE CONfused with the Asphodel Meadows.

MAP YOUR ROUTE

34

MOST OF AZRAEL'S EYES WERE A BROWNISH black but some were blue and others yellow. Their pupils were heart-shaped, crescents, slits. Cones pulsed behind them. All of them could rest while open and watch while shut and they saw everything that moved or was about to move or had ceased to move. Azrael remembered when the first one appeared on his body. It was near his nipple. It became his nipple. It gazed at him and neither was afraid. Azrael then was a mere calf, kid, spiderling, lamb. What was there to fear?

NIPPLE

35

AS A TODDLER SHE HAD CAUSED A SENSATION in her family when she announced she wanted to live in a little hole like the ant. Not an ant, *the* ant. This might have been misheard.

She was an easygoing child, not particularly thoughtful and stubbornly inartistic. Her temperament was not in the least unruly or mystical. But when she was fourteen she was struck in the head by a surfboard and almost drowned. In a matter of moments she became an NDEer, a member of that serene and suspect tribe of tinsley-like persuasion. Attempting to articulate her near-death experience she found it differed scarcely at all from thousands of other accounts. There was the light, the empty road, the endless shore, the light, the tunnel, the ascent, the view of the unimportant body below. The feeling of limitlessness, oneness, freedom, the sudden dismay at the obstruction, the shut door, the check, the thwart, the cruel boundary. Then the turning back, the forced retreat, the unpleasant feeling of being drawn down a kind of funnel, a cone . . .

A therapist told her that she'd experienced a depersonalization which is basically a psychological defense against death. The mind has many wiles.

I still feel that way, she said. Depersonalized. Like, whatever.

She wondered if she would see it again, that shining threshold, when it really mattered.

ANT

36

HE'D BEEN DIAGNOSED WITH A CANCER THAT was metastasizing rapidly. He was fifteen years of age and naturally he was pissed. As his disease progressed, his parents disgusted him more and more. He couldn't help it. They were broken to him, his mother especially who wept continuously. He told them he wanted a Firebird for his birthday, a first generation Pontiac Firebird. They found one for him quickly and it was delivered on a flatbed. It had been lovingly restored. The color was Blizzard Pearl. Radical.

His father was too anxious to give him driving lessons so an instructor was hired. He was of the know-where-your-vehicle-is-in-space-and-place-at-all-times school, the bump-the-cone school. You practice with the cones, trying to bump them at first over and over as you're backing up or pulling ahead until you can't. You couldn't hit them if you tried. It would be offensive to your new knowledge of space and place. The cones taught him a lot, he felt, maybe everything he needed to know.

STRIKING STYLE

37

WHEN AZRAEL WAS AN INFANT CUB COLT PUP gosling, before tongues and eyes began covering his form and wings commenced to appear, each one more splendid than the one preceding, he had many questions, but after he met God only a few remained.

THE MEETING

38

I HAVE A REQUEST, SHE SAID.

OK.

I wish to be buried with my horse.

He was shocked. He's not even dead, he said. He knew this sounded stupid because she wasn't dead yet either. This was the near future they were talking about. He's still fresh, he ain't but three years old, he added. It just seems a little mean.

You have to promise me.

You don't ride him that much, he said, troubled.

Because I can't! I've been sick. I'm very sick.

All right, all right, don't get excited.

She kept changing the horse's name. He supposed that wasn't bad. It's boats you're not supposed to change the name. It's boats where that's unlucky.

Did you have a dream or something?

It's a vision. It comforts me. Why won't you promise!

OK, OK, he said. Don't worry about it then. One less thing to worry about.

One less thing, she said.

COME ALONG

39

WHEN HE WAS IN ONE OF HIS BLUE PERIODS, the Devil feared that he had lost his edge, that alien awareness that sees matters differently, that thinks differently. That it was gone. And what remained had been embraced, enthusiastically embraced by the predictably human, the tares that made up his unholy aggregate. They were perennially hungry and impatient, they were boring. He couldn't stand most of his followers, they were bums. And there were so many of them, it would appear that he had won. But he didn't want to win, he wanted to keep playing the game.

TARES

40

VLADIMIR NABOKOV WHEN HE WAS DYING had tears in his eyes. In this he was not the first. His son Dimitri said that those tears indicated to him that his father had come to realize that he would never again pursue his beloved butterflies, that they were on the wing without him. This was true. He would die and be no longer capable of experiencing the joy of stalking—the capture, extinguishment and analysis. He had once referred to the forests and fields of mid-century America as his "collecting grounds." Who knows how many butterflies he lovingly excitedly executed—his collections are all over the place.

The butterfly has long been the symbol of recovery, rebirth, metamorphosis, the arising of the soul. Such baggage was rubbish to Nabokov. He was mostly interested in the radiant insects' genitalia. Such minute and improbable perfection. If he hadn't become a writer he would have been a lepidopterist, he said.

CAREER

41

SPEAKING OF BUTTERFLIES, THE DEVIL SAID, I saw an image of you the other day crushing one with your winged foot.

That was not me.

Angel of Death. It was captioned quite clearly.

Death and I are not the same.

A difference without distinction, the Devil said.

Oh please stop, Azrael said. The butterfly being crushed is some gnostic invention. Their behavior is difficult to interpret properly.

That one's pretty obvious but they can be somewhat abstruse, the Devil granted. They dwell on the origin of evil overmuch but they can be fun. They've dispensed with a great deal of fluff. No forgiveness, no miracles, don't have to love your neighbor. And you've got to admit their portrayal of the little children dwelling in the field that's not theirs is pretty cool. They're not concerned with what one does but with what one knows.

I've got to go, Azrael said gloomily.

But before he left he said, I know you know I'm not Death.

THOSE GNOSTICS

42

HIS THOUGHTS WERE TURNING MORE AND more to how he wanted to dispose of the body—his own, which pleased him less with each passing year. Casket burial was unsuitable and cremation wasn't much better as it contributed so heavily to aerial pollution. He considered being composted and decided to tour a recently licensed facility. There he was shown the hexagon shaped vessels, the cones and cylinders, the curing bins, even the resultant product, a lovely cubic foot of loam.

The process is completely driven by microbes, an intern said. Six to ten weeks total. And it's up to you if you want to be placed in one of our forests or park-like sites or be returned to friends or family for use in their gardens. Special trees or rose beds can be a cherished choice . . .

The interns were used to the stunned looks people exhibited touring this place. God knows what they were thinking.

Seldom mentioned was that occasionally in these ecological death operations the resultant product is found to be not ideal as nourishing compost. Something is awry in the chemical composition of the stuff and it ends up being employed in the less flattering but still necessary business of erosion control. The interns, who were just kids for the most part, called these situations, which happened frequently actually, FTRs. Failure to Recompense.

RECOMPENSE

43

OF THE MANY HUNDREDS OF EGYPTIAN gods, Anubis and Thoth were the most elegantly paired. One black, one white, with the head of a jackal and an ibis respectively. They worked well together for centuries, then overnight it seemed, though that was an illusion, they became dispensable, victims of their own strict protocol. Their dealings were with the deceased and they determined who would qualify to take the next step into the bountiful afterlife. For this to occur, the individual's heart could not weigh more than a single feather. People began to reckon that this was virtually impossible. Modifications to the rule were made and it was determined that careful mummification would assure passage. Anubis became more specifically identified with the mortuary arts.

STILL NOT FOR EVERYONE

44

THE DEVIL DREAMED HE WAS A TOOTH, AN extraordinarily large tooth, harboring an immense cavity.

He spoke of this dream to Azrael.

Was this upon awakening? Azrael inquired. I realize you never sleep but I have to ask anyway.

The Devil affirmed it was upon awakening that he felt he was a tooth.

That was the beginning of the dream then, Azrael said.

I believe it was the end. One doesn't awaken when one's just begun.

You dream a dream according to one order and remember it in another, Azrael said calmly. To make it more comprehensible.

Is that so! the Devil exclaimed.
Do you find me perceptive? Azrael asked.
No, the Devil said. You are creative.
Oh. OK. Thank you.
I mean, you're not really taking them anywhere.

TOOTH

45

WASHOE, CHIMP WHO LEARNED SIGN LANGUAGE
dies at 42 without signing goodbye.

DISAPPOINTING

Newspaper headline
Oct. 30, 2007

46

"Here, Father, here!"

HERE, FATHER, HERE

*Thomas Wolfe

47

AZRAEL KNOWS THAT THE DEVIL DOESN'T take him seriously. You don't even know how to converse, the Devil says. And it's true. Azrael is mostly silent whereas the Devil likes to engage in long conversations, usually gay and inconsequential but not always. The Devil talks to everyone except himself. God, despite the rumors, never enters into dialogue with anyone. The Devil likes games and mazes. He is forever inventing new mazes, more and more difficult to solve, three-dimensional ones, four . . . The amusement of the maze is the height of secularity. Azrael prefers labyrinths which the Devil finds comically sentimental and predictable. Azrael has also expressed his affection for desert places. He likes the mystique of deserts, their harboring of prophets, their solemnity and stern disdainful beauty. And the ravens! Who appear out of nowhere. First One. And then another to form a gleaming pair. They are the only birds not alarmed by his presence. But the Devil points out that it's been a long while since deserts birthed a prophet and they've become like so many of earth's once confounding regions—exploited, ravaged and ultimately put to death. The Devil doesn't bother going to deserts anymore. As for the ravens, he suspects that they must find Azrael . . . winsome. At best.

RAVEN ONE AND RAVEN TWO

48

SHE WANTED HER BIB TO BE CRISP AND CLEAN and she wished to be served with all the solemnity of communion after a rousing sermon on one of the bleaker lessons. The time, preferably twilight. A manhattan would be ideal of course but she understood the potion offered would not at all taste like a manhattan. She should prepare herself to find it bitter, even burning. Still she held out hope that she would experience it as something dignified and darkly fulsome. Classic. Legendary.

MATCHLESS

49

EVERY ONCE IN AWHILE A SOUL WOULD SHRIEK as though she hadn't forgotten she'd just experienced death and was reliving it as it were. This occurred when Azrael and Death appeared simultaneously which was as rare as it was undesirable. Death had innumerable wardrobes and guises Azrael suspected but whenever he encountered the great Thanatos, Death appeared as lichen.

When he confided this to the Devil, the Devil considered it not particularly peculiar. Lichens are mysteriously complex. They come in peace and are theoretically immortal.

I find it absolutely marvelous that you see Death as lichen, the Devil said, laughing. It really is so you.

LICHEN

50

WHEN SHE WAS A CHILD THEY DROVE IN THE spring over a mountain to visit her grandmother. It was called Bear Mountain and at its peak was a gas station and a bear in a cage. Once the mountain had all belonged to the bear and her family.

The bear wore a chain that she dragged back and forth across her allowance. Bits of oranges were scattered about her but they were not nice oranges. She had once had children, where were her children . . .

She had loved seeing the bear, aware that she was somehow misperceiving the situation. But she recognized a mystery and was greedy for it. It was the high point of the journey and the coming back too.

On these visits in the spring, her parents slept downstairs on a sofa in her grandmother's house and she slept upstairs on a bed with her grandmother, an arrangement she did not like. At the bottom of the yard there was an outhouse. It was very clean, her grandmother kept it immaculate. She lived alone, she did everything herself.

At some point in college, the child grown, she had taken the time to write in her textbook on 17th century prose—*The magical lines in Donne's poetry are those which awake such conceptions as those of space time nothingness and eternity.*

Now here she was, ill, aching, old, older than her grandmother had been when she died, older than her parents had been as well, wondering what she had ever wondered about.

The bear had always looked past her, not seeing her at all, not caring in the slightest that she would sometimes appear.

GOD'S VIZAR

51

PYTHAGORAS, WHO NEVER WROTE ANYTHING down, is considered an expert on the soul after death.

He also invented a joke drinking cup, copies of which are still sold in Aegean gift shops today.

PASS THE ENVELOPE

52

WHAT I FIND IMPRESSIVE, THE DEVIL SAID, IS that you're neither canonical or noncanonical. That's a remarkable balancing act. Good for you. But aren't you supposed to have a book? A great book wherein you scribble down names and erase them constantly?

That's just a tale. I couldn't do that with everything else I'm supposed to do, Azrael said defensively.

The Devil was always teasing him for his lack of independence. You are utterly under His command. And you take only the souls He commands you to take.

That's still a lot, Azrael said.

What's your attitude toward metempsychosis?

I am so fond of metempsychosis! Azrael said eagerly. I wish I could do that exclusively. But times have changed so. The possibilities just aren't there anymore.

Other forms of being becoming unavailable are they? Extreme Biodiversity loss? Species winking out right and left. 70% of this gone. 70% of that. It adds up.

Sadness descended upon Azrael. His many eyes closed for a moment. His feathers trembled.

But I must have faith that this is intended, he thought.

DISTURBING ARITHMETIC

53

IT WAS JUST A LITTLE STRETCH OF HIGHWAY outside Gallup, less than a mile stretch and before her appeared the bodies of all the horses and dogs and Diné that had been struck and killed there—their ghost bodies. It was disturbing. No one had ever mentioned such a phenomena. She had to navigate through this multitude carefully. It took every bit of her concentration. Then it was over. It was as though she'd emerged from a tunnel. She had been on her way to buy some silver bracelets with coral inlays and was hoping she could acquire them for less than they were being offered. She thought for a moment that she would not buy them at all. But that would be silly.

THE CONSEQUENCES OF HISTORY

54

DEEP IN THE CAVE, FRESCOES ON THE CEILING were pointed out to visitors. You weren't supposed to shine light upon them but the guide said he would, just for an instant. The pictures were primitive, faded almost to nothing. Following a line where water had once flowed in the rock, fish were swimming.

TOUR

55

ARE ANY OF THOSE EYES OF YOURS TETRAR-chromatic? the Devil asked. He was putting drops in his own which had been bothering him of late. His eyes were the most extraordinary indigo color. He was vain about that too.

I believe all of them are, Azrael said.

That's nice, the Devil said.

THE FOURTH CONE

56

BLAISE PASCAL. THE BRILLIANT MATHEMATICIAN loved triangles, vacuums, hexagrams and wheels, cycloids and conics, even the degenerate ones which fail to be an irreducible curve. He thought in the manner of divine geometries. He was a genius and sickly. He seldom ate unless fed by his loving family in drops and spoonfuls. He probably had terrible headaches. When he was thirty-one he experienced what he called a "night of fire" though it only lasted two hours—between 10:30 in the evening until half past midnight. Oddly enough, this mystical event did not appear to him as shapes. He transposed the hours, more or less coherently, to words on a bit of paper. The words were nothing extraordinary. *Certitude. God.*

Feeling Joy Peace Jesus. Tears of Joy. It is said that he sewed the paper into his coat so that this tangible evidence of the grace bestowed upon him that night could be with him in this foul dimension. He never returned to mathematics or her sister, physics, but spent his remaining years—there were eight of them—composing his *Pensées*—reflections on God, meaning, and the faith that transcends the limitations of thought. He collected these notes, these pensées into "bundles." No order in which they were to be read was provided—neither within a "bundle" or between various "bundles." The beauty of this is these fragments are not based on logic, though mathematics is not based on logic either. Nothing is based on logic.

THE 23RD OF NOVEMBER

57

ROBERT LOWELL, ON WRITING A POEM ABOUT the death of the family's guinea pig, Mrs. Muffin, was moved to quote Heidegger.

TIME IS ECSTASY

58

AZRAEL COULD PICTURE THE DEVIL AS A cherub, not as fashionably perceived putti, a pinkly pudgy child of saccharine expression, but the unadulterated terrifying original, a being with the head of four creaturely faces embodied in the whirling light of a wheel spinning within a wheel.

The Devil couldn't look like that anymore, God made sure of that. But Azrael was quite aware of the cherubin and the Devil had once been counted the most trusted of their number guarding the peculiarly named mercy seat and the Supreme I Am Itself.

It was so tedious, the Devil said. Praise Praise Praise was a required constant. It was Yes Yes Yes, Your Endlessness, day and night. We gained some respect when we were described but then confusion followed, that never should have happened . . .

Confusion?

The baby thing. The cuteness. And such irrelevant duties were added. At one point the cherubim were urged to be kindly confessors. There is nothing remotely absolving about those wheels! Everything became diluted.

But you were gone by then.

Yes, I was in the beginning only. I was the brightest one. I was never replaced.

You're irreplaceable, Azrael ventured.

Thank you, the Devil said. You're very kind.

BRIGHTEST

59

GOD ORIGINALLY WANTED MUSLIMS TO PRAY fifty times a day. When Moses heard about this during Muhammad's Night Journey he pronounced the number ridiculous. He insisted that Muhammad negotiate whereupon the number was reduced to five which Moses thought was still too many. But Muhammad didn't want to argue the matter further and there it stands: one prays upon awakening, when the sun is precisely overhead, in midafternoon, at sunset, and before sleep.

ONLY SENSIBLE

60

THEY MUST JUST AVOID, BY FLYING HIGHER and higher, the tiny ruthless figures with their incomprehensible purpose massed in the fields below.

MIGRATION

61

WOULD YOU LIKE TO LISTEN TO A BIT OF BACH together? the Devil inquired. St. John's Passion again, I suppose?

We can listen to St. Matthew's. It's your turn I think.

No quite all right. I like the St. John's well enough. My favorite part of the oratorio is the jabber of the priests and lawyers. Those sneering violins!

He began preparing the records for his impressive turntable. I've heard, he said, that sometimes you appear as an old woman. Is that correct?

Yes, Azrael said. But I almost never do anymore. It alarms them terribly. To tell you the truth witnessing anything human in that instant succeeding death is the last thing anybody wants.

HahahaHA, the Devil said.

HE ALONE DECIDES WHO
WRITES A SYMPHONY

**He*: American hymn

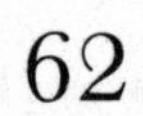

ROOM 111

&

ROOM 112

63

THEY FLED THE FIRE THAT HAD ALREADY consumed twenty thousand acres with two parrots, a sixty-year-old tortoise and three dogs, Bunny, Frank and King. They were so grateful they had made it out together.

ATHEISTS OUGHT NOT TO BE
OFFERING CONSOLATION
EITHER.

*Christopher Hitchens

64

THE SOUL IS IMMORTAL BUT NOT INDESTRUCtible.

Yeah, I get that.

You do?

Yeah, that's not hard.

To get?

To understand. It's pretty fundamental.

I don't believe you. I think you're pretending to understand.

Let's get out of here and have some drinks at Barb's Wire.

I hate Barb's Wire. Place is filthy.

What do you have against it?

I just told you.

We can continue our conversation there.

No. I'm done. Anyone who thinks it's perfectly acceptable that the soul is immortal but not indestructible isn't the one for me.

I didn't say that. What kind of fool would think it was perfectly acceptable?

ON THE ROCKS

65

ON A JOURNEY, TRAVELING ALONE, HE became ill.

He was in an old hotel that someone was ambitiously renovating. He was a guest here but had not been invited. That was the way these arrangements were made and accepted but it suddenly struck him as strange. Outside, an enormous sun was going down.

He undressed, turned back the coverlet and got into the high wide bed. He could not remember falling asleep but he woke violently, trembling with chills and fever. He fell from the bed and lay nauseous on the polished wooden floor. Beneath the bed was a tented sticky trap for roaches. It harbored a single roach whose antennae delicately waved and probed the air. The antennae of the roach constantly keeps it informed, prevents it from becoming disoriented. They determine which direction could possibly be taken, whether the predator is close or farther away. They seek and sense what lies ahead. They search, from any quarter, a way forward.

His knowledge of the roach's predicament was sudden, complete and dreadful. With effort he swung himself away from the sight and curled naked in a corner. His limbs shook, his eyes stung and his throat was dry. He thought it might be the soup he'd eaten. He could see the kitchen from where he'd been sitting earlier at the café counter. The pots were old and black. The stove was black. Nothing was shining back there certainly. Still, he had eaten the soup, or most of it, and it had tasted all right.

CERIDWEN

66

WHAT DO THE RICH HAVE TO LOOK FORWARD to after death? Nothing!

SO THERE

*Luke 12:19–20

67

YOU HAVE MINIONS, AZRAEL SAID.

So many, the Devil said. But I prefer to call them satellites. Quick! Is the moon a satellite?

Startled, Azrael said no.

It is a satellite, the Devil said gravely. Earth's satellite. It controls the tides.

Well I do know that, Azrael said, embarrassed.

It maintains order. The seasons and such.

Spring, Azrael mused.

But not for much longer.

Is that true! Azrael exclaimed.

It will not tolerate forever human beings' rude assaults—the probing and prodding and poking and collecting.

Misguided, Azrael said.

Have these people *ever* known what they were looking for? the Devil demanded.

Then he smiled. Azrael often made the foul fiend smile. He was so innocent, so eternally, newly fledged. And the Devil knew exactly what he was thinking. He was wondering if it could be mercifully forgotten that he didn't know the moon was a satellite.

MOON CONVERSATION

68

ALL THE BUSTED STUFF OR STUFF WE DON'T want anymore we put in the front yard under the tarp. Technically there is no backyard but we call the space on the street the front yard all the same. Everything eventually goes under the tarp. My grandpa won't take it to the dump. He says: "Why should I engage Rosie in such a hopeless enterprise?" He calls his vehicle Rosie from a song—*she ain't pretty, she ain't small, ain't no fairy tale ain't no skin and bones but* . . . dah dah dah . . .

My mother would plant a garden in that space she says. Tomatoes, squash, corn, maybe flowers, roses even. The tarp would be removed and the yard would be wonderous. "Where you gonna put the tarp then," my grandpa says. "There'd be no place to put it when it's unnecessary." The tarp's been there as long as I can remember and it's a strong one, tied down good. When the wind and dust storms rip through town the tarp does not succumb. It has never succumbed. After a storm, the first thing we do is see if the tarp has held up and it always has.

The land outside the town looks empty and it is. It's not that I'm just not noticing something that's there. My mother worries about my imagination. She believes I should have one and worries that I don't. "An imagination tides you children over until you're grown," she says. "It gets you through the day."

"I don't need no babysitter," I say.

"Of course not," she says. "I'm talking about imagination, more of a friend."

But my mind feels webby and hard. Even grandpa and Rosie don't bother going into that barren land anymore.

"Was there something out there once?" I ask.

"Oh yes," my mother says, "so many lovely things."

69

PHOSPHOGYPSUM IS THE MOST RADIOACTIVE waste left over from processing phosphate ore into fertilizer. For every ton of fertilizer, the industry produces five tons of acidic carcinogenic byproduct. This is stored in stacks hundreds of acres wide and hundreds of feet tall and in vast lined holding ponds which fill up with stormwater runoff and rainfall even when the facility has long since ceased processing ore which was the case in the sunny state of Florida on the shores of Tampa Bay, an estuary of the Gulf of Mexico. Communities had been built near the abandoned plant, car repair and coffee shops, doctors' offices, all manner of amenities. These would be befouled should the stacks and ponds fail and disgorge their fatal muck.

A new port being dredged to accommodate supertankers might also be compromised by delays. The ponds did begin to leak and fail and it was determined that the best way to avoid an uncontrollable catastrophe was to release two hundred million gallons or so of the poison into the waters of Tampa Bay where Mother Nature would be counted upon to do her best in the dispersing and diluting department. Aquatic life began to visibly perish within a few weeks. Forty tons of dead fish, fifty tons, sixty. Manatee populations crashed. Someone said: "If it's swimming in the bay now it's washing up dead." But he wasn't a scientist, he was just an ordinary person expressing his opinion to a journalist. Scientists would never speak in such a crude generality. They were monitoring the situation and would continue to monitor the situation. That's what they do in these circumstances.

FERTILIZER

70

THE OCEANS WERE BEING DESALINIZED SO people could be clean and have ice and grow food and poppies and drink it as well. They needed fresh water and didn't have it anymore. The oceans were vast, they covered 70% of the planet. The thinking went: first eradication, then development. The argument would be: nothing lives there anymore. There was more plastic in the ocean than fish.

Some of Azrael's eyes were closed. Fewer than a hundred but still worrisome. They were not encrusted or inflamed, just shut, firmly shut. Was it rebellion? He didn't know how to talk to his eyes. He lapped the shut ones a little with a tongue. Nothing but a slight salt taste. Had they been weeping?

He had taken the souls of octopi and sharks, great fishes and rays and turtles, even the glittering lowly ones, the little ones. Such transport was not believed but it was true. They too were permitted to wait in the hidden retreat, but unlike humankind they would fear no further judgment.

SALT

71

YOU KNOW THE STORY OF THE GREAT WRITER Tolstoy and his experience in a little room where he was spending the night on his way from one place to another don't you?

Well, it was a simple square whitewashed room, with one small window with a red curtain. It felt sad to Tolstoy, terribly sad. Even worse, he felt an intense horror in the little room, a spiritual nausea. He wrote:

Why had I decided to stop here? Where am I taking myself? From what and where to am I running? I'm running from something frightful that I can't escape . . . I stepped out into the hallway, hoping to leave behind that which was tormenting me. But it came out after me . . . I was just as scared, more scared even.

What nonsense, I said to myself. Why do I feel anguish, what am I scared of?

Of me, came the soundless voice of death. I am here . . .

And everything was different for him after that. His life, his writing, everything.

THE WITHDRAWING ROOM

72

WHEN SHE WAS ABOUT AN HOUR AWAY SHE'D called the house sitter and said she'd be arriving soon.

"I broke a few things," the girl said. "Accidentally of course but might as well tell you now."

"Oh," she said. She'd been informed by her only a few days ago that one of the fish had died, the big one, the little one still seemed fine. "Are you all right," she'd said, confused.

"Sure," the girl said.

"How is Jim?" Jim was her Bernese Mountain Dog. After she'd purchased him, she was told the breed wasn't particularly loyal, ranked quite low in that department actually, but she found him loyal enough. What did that mean, even?

"He's at the pound. He bit some kid. I told them I was sure he'd had his rabies shot but it was like nobody believed me. It's good you'll be back soon."

"How on earth did he find a kid?" she said half-humorously. "Jim just stays in the house, the yard."

"I had some friends over. They all have kids, which is hardly abnormal."

She hung up the phone and set the cruise control to seventy-five. The girl's tone was . . . her tone was certainly unacceptable. She was a former student. She barely remembered her when she first showed up but now was in the habit of hiring her to watch the house when she traveled. She hadn't been one of her more interesting students though she was certain, more or less certain, that she had never told her she was utterly without talent.

BIG FISH LITTLE FISH

73

THERE ARE 42 PSALMS OF LAMENT IN THE Hebrew Bible, eight of which are communal. They all possess a certain structure. There is the Cry, followed by Confession of Trust, the Petition, the Exclamation of Certainty and the Vow of Praise. Some can also include a curse on the enemies which the people believe to be the cause of their suffering or a claiming of the people's innocence in the situation.

INCLUDE IF HELPFUL

74

IS THAT TREE STILL THERE DO YOU KNOW? the Devil asked.

No, Azrael said.

Now hold on, you're not even going to ask which one?

I know the one you mean, Azrael said.

It was the great tree that grows below the throne of God. Each leaf has the name of a person on it and when the leaf detaches itself and commences to drop through the air, slowly, slowly, that person would have forty days remaining of the only life they'd ever be aware of.

So what happened to it?

They went up as high as they could and cut the roots.

What madness!

You had nothing to do with this?

I? Certainly not. I have always admired trees and the way they exist in an extra dimension. If any more are cut down the earth will be terminally unhealed by the rain's convulsions.

This one was quite extraordinary.

And what it offered was such a tender courtesy, the Devil sighed. No one appreciates the little kindnesses anymore. You'd think the idiots would have been grateful that their foolish names were being acknowledged at all.

COURTESY

75

DANTE, BEFORE HE ASCENDS THE MOUNTAINS of Purgatory is told that his face must be cleansed of the tears he shed in Hell and Virgil washes his face with dew.

DEW AGAIN

76

JUNG DREAMED A GREAT DEAL ABOUT THE dead, the land of the dead and the rising of the dead. As a schoolboy he developed an embarrassing tendency to faint when pressured or when he was being teased. In the winter of 1925 when he was around fifty, he visited the American West. The anthropologist, linguist and hipster Jaime de Angulo told him to meet him at the Grand Canyon and from there they traveled to Taos, New Mexico. Also in the touring party was Fowler McCormick, son of Cyrus, the reaping machine inventor, and grandson of John D. Rockefeller. There in the pueblo, Jung was introduced to a man described as a Hopi elder whose anglicized name was somewhat erroneously translated as "Mountain Lake."

The two sat on one of the roofs of the pueblo and watched the sun move across the sky. It was January and must have been very cold.

By all accounts Jung had a marvelous time though he learned little about Indian spiritual life. "Never before had I run into such an atmosphere of secrecy," he noted while lamenting that "the religions of civilized nations today are all accessible, their sacraments have long ago ceased to be mysteries." He longed to be introduced to something new.

After his visit he attempted to correspond with Mountain Lake. "Any information you can give me about your religious life is always welcome," he wrote.

CARL

77

THEY DO KNOW THAT THEIR SOULS DON'T belong to them anymore after they die, right? The souls become impersonal, non-individual. They do know that's the deal, right?

Everything's different. They're prepared for that, I believe.

Prepared for everything being different, I doubt it, the Devil said. But let's just think about this for a moment. Souls are non-particular but they're awaiting the resurrection of the body from which they've been expelled?

Their condition is not one of waiting.

The soul's afterlife is assured but it's not a personal afterlife. It's not connected to life.

I can't . . . I'm not wise enough to explain.

You're not meant to explain.

No.

You're meant for something else. I don't believe this re-birthday surprise has been thoroughly thought through.

May I have a drink?

Why certainly, the Devil exclaimed, what shall we have?

A milkshake, Azrael said.

A milkshake!

I don't want anything! I just wish you wouldn't hound me like this. I wish you'd be distracted.

You know what crows wish for, I assume, the Devil said playfully, easing up.

Yes.

Nigredo. That's what they are. Primigenial.

Yes, crows are marvelous. Crows and ravens.

Azrael was glad he and his difficult friend could agree on something.

Same genus. Like spirit and soul, the Devil concluded with satisfaction.

THE CROW WISHES

EVERYTHING WAS BLACK

78

NIETZSCHE HAD MANY THOUGHTS BUT HE maintained that the thought of thoughts was recurrence.

PASTURE

*John 10:9

79

THE DEVIL HAD AN INFINITE SUPPLY OF sneakers and never wore the same pair twice as far as Azrael could tell.

You know the reason we had the great falling out was because I wasn't supportive of that Adam and Eve business.

I'd heard that. It was a mistake you think.

The proof is in the pudding.

I can imagine you must miss Him still.

Oh we remain tight as ticks.

Why are you speaking so strangely, Azrael said, concerned.

I'm tired. I'm running down.

You mean you feel run-down?

Yes, that's it. You know what He told me? I might as well share it with you. He said: The existence of creatures and their non-existence are the same.

He said that?

Admitted it, yes.

He sounds a little tired too.

No, no, He's always saying that, the Devil said.

A LITTLE TIRED

80

THE DESTITUTE SIBLINGS GEORGE AND ANDER made the bit of money they did by picking blueberries in the summer and in the winter making wreaths which were known for their messiness. They were hardly even circular which is the one requirement of a wreath—that it should be perfectly circular as a symbol of eternal life. The old brothers were meticulous berry pickers—clean, no leaves or twigs in the buckets—this disparity in approach between the only two actions they ever undertook was frequently noted. Still, people liked the imperfect wreaths which adorned many doors well into spring when blueberry season was just around the corner.

ONE SANG IN CHURCH AND ONE DIDN'T. IT WAS THE ONLY WAY YOU COULD TELL THEM APART.

81

SHE WAS GIVEN A PENCIL AND A SHEAF OF pages. After much consideration she drew on one of the pages and offered it to them.

They seemed to have the long talons of birds and they swept the talons across a stone and a single spark rose toward the paper and consumed it.

She bent over another page and the same procedure was followed.

She continued, ever more slowly and with greater care. Apparently it was permissible to recall and return all that she had sought to cherish on this earth.

LOSS OF HABITAT

82

THE DEVIL HAD LITTLE TO OCCUPY HIS TIME which had become less and less valuable. Everything he stood for was running along on its own, requiring very little involvement on his part. He had his snakes to care for but the truth was they didn't want his care. His association with them had made their lives extremely difficult. They were feared and harassed, incessantly murdered even though their existence underground kept the earth from falling apart, something people once knew but didn't anymore. Snakes were so interesting and tragic—dethroned kings—he really admired them but they wanted nothing to do with him. He had quite inadvertently betrayed them.

HIBERNACULUM

83

AZRAEL WAS LOOKING AT THE DEVIL'S SNAKES through a great glass window.

How they coil in endless unity, Azrael marveled.

They don't like me, the Devil said.

I'm sure that's not the case, Azrael said kindly. They're just not emotive. He waved at the snakes through the glass.

See, they don't respond to me either.

The Devil regarded him sourly.

Azrael peered at the patterned, glowing folds. Are there any in there with the hood?

Oh you are such a child! the Devil exclaimed. The hood, honestly, such drama!

But the hood is so rad, Azrael thought.

SUCH FLAIR

84

THE MANAGER WAS TALKING TO HIS FIANCÉE about an employee who was always screwing up. They were sitting in an empty restaurant and he was becoming agitated about this employee.

"She's so incompetent. I ask her to copy something and she'll come back with blank pages. She's always forgetting to give me messages."

"She sounds so incompetent."

"She used to drink heavily but she hasn't had a drink in six years now."

"Six years is nothing," the fiancée said.

"I went against my better judgment when I hired her. She had no experience in office work. She's spent some time in jail." He seemed on the verge of screaming.

"Just fire her."

"But she doesn't have any money. I pay her well but she tells me she doesn't know where it goes. She'll always be pulling the devil by the tail."

"She sounds so dumb."

"You know what her response is when I confront her? Like I say, 'Jesus, Kathy, this mail should have gone out last week.'"

"I don't. I'm kind of incurious too."

"She says, 'Sorry.' That's it." He shook his head. "She killed her child."

"What!" the fiancée gasped.

"One of them. She didn't mean to of course. She was driving drunk and there was an accident. That's the reason she was in jail."

"Oh my God," the fiancée said. She felt disoriented. She needed some food or something. Had she ordered brussel sprouts again? They were good in this place but she worried about them sticking to her teeth.

"Did I order?" she asked him.

"Have we ordered yet? I don't think we've ordered," he said.

PULL

85

THE YAQUI, AN INDIGENOUS TRIBE OF THE state of Sonora in Mexico and southwestern Arizona, have access to many worlds. These overlapping worlds—*aniam*—are the worlds of animals, night, dreams, people, flowers, death . . . There are many others. The complex mythology of the Yaquis is most beautifully rendered in the Deer Dance. The deer comes from *yo ania*—the enchanted world, enters the *hyua ania*, the wilderness world and dances in the *sea ania*, the flower world. The ritual of the dance weaves the worlds and eliminates the evil done by man. It can also be quite the burlesque. It is performed on special days and during Pascua—Easter.

An old story of the Yaquis and one that can be told concerns two hunters walking in the desert with powerful rifles. They saw a small deer in the distance looking at them curiously. One of them shot the deer which fell, mortally wounded. But immediately the animal rose, shook off the dirt and regarded them as before. The deer was shot and struck again and once more after thrashing about in the dirt, rose intact in the same spot and gazed at them. For the third time, the little deer, the *soutela,* was shot and collapsed in an enormous cloud of dust. When this cleared, the deer was standing, watching them. It then disappeared. The men finally realized or were later informed, that the deer came from the *yo ania* and wanted to offer them wisdom but they had refused to accept it.

When the Yaquis were first introduced to Christianity they found the story stupefying and did not think it brought good news.

NEWS

86

THE NIGHT SEEMED DARKER THAN USUAL.

No light pollution here, the Devil said contentedly. Would you like to translate Hadrian's little poem again with me?

All right, Azrael said.

Revisiting the great pagan on his deathbed addressing his soul and fearing for its future was one of the Devil's favorite things.

Animula vagula blandula
Hospes comesque corporis
Quae nunc abibis in loca
Pallidula rigida nudula
Nec ut soles dabis iocos

Countless had been the versions of these five simple lines.

Borne on thy vagrant pinion . . . Was that you or someone else?

Someone else, Azrael said.

Petted stray? Funny darling? Poor wanderer? Beloved vagrant?

Vagrant, no. That word wouldn't have occurred to me.

Soul as squatter in the temple of the body. Ugh, the Devil said.

Azrael was always eager to confront the poem's challenge but then quickly felt something very much like alarm.

I've found, the Devil said, that you have the most trouble describing what awaits the little drifter which is odd don't you think given your role in all this . . .

87

THEY'D BEEN MARRIED FOR FIFTY YEARS. No children, eleven cars, five houses, two DUIs, three infidelities, ten dogs. Innumerable breakfasts and cocktails. The Christmas trees could be counted, the putting up and the taking down, and the ornaments, carefully removed from their nests then replaced. The summers too—those were the years when summers were a world apart.

"Oh my dear, my dear," he said. He stood by her bedside in the hospital. Their friends didn't think his being there was a good idea. He'd actually been brought over from another institution. He suffered dementia, it wasn't Alzheimer's, he'd been assured. He had thick hair still, beautiful hair and large forthright ears.

A nurse brought water in cone shaped paper cups. One was to drink it quickly, then the cup was discarded. This was understood. One couldn't linger, holding it, or place it aside with its small offer of refreshment to be appreciated at a later time.

"Oh my dear, my dear, I hate leaving you like this," he said.

She knew what he meant. They smiled quite blindly at one another. She was going to die! Her body knew it. It was amazing. Yet she was unalarmed. The trick was not to think you're yourself.

A LEOPARD CAME OUT OF THE SEA AND SANK BACK DOWN. BUT PATIENCE, PATIENCE.

*Elizabeth Hardwick
Sleepless Nights

88

RILKE ONCE REFERRED TO HIS PENIS—THE poet's penis—as a womb-dazzling rocket.

The Angels weren't indifferent to him, the Devil thought. They just didn't like him.

WHO IF I CRIED WOULD HEAR
ME AMONG THE ANGELIC ORDERS?

*René

89

I HAVE FOUND, THE DEVIL SAID, THAT THE feeling that the end is near has abated among human beings.

It seems so, yes, Azrael said.

Don't you find it strange? When the end in fact is so very near?

Perhaps their concept of time has changed.

Concept of time! Whatever can you mean! You seem a little preoccupied this evening.

A rather odd thing happened to me if I may be bold enough to say. It's not related to what we're discussing though I don't think.

That's all right, the Devil said.

Well I arrived and this fellow's inkings were seething. They had covered every millimeter of his body and they had managed to free themselves and were hovering there, very upset at the situation.

Had they no inkling?

Apparently not.

The inkings had no inkling, the Devil howled.

The soul was not present.

Subsumed? the Devil asked, calm again.

I don't know. It certainly wasn't there. It was as if the tattoos had nibbled it to nothing. It was gone.

Oh that's a good one, the Devil said.

END RESULT

90

COULD IT BE THAT SOULS ARE LEAVING A person before the body dies? Azrael wondered.

Certainly. Why not? the Devil said. Get out of that grub-case. Why wait until the last minute.

I've been noticing a falling off in the customary process.

The Devil yawned in comfortable abandon. He had no fear of Evil entering him when he did. He enjoyed yawning. He finally settled and looked at Azrael sympathetically. It was inevitable, he said. The soul wants out. Not being fed what's necessary. Requires a better host. Why stick around . . .

But where can they go? Azraël said fretfully. Nature's vesture is no longer available. Indwelling anywhere there is impossible. The mountains have been stripped of their holiness, the oceans of their mysteries.

Azrael looked so anguished that the Devil said formally, Truly, I take no pleasure in this. But privately he thought, mice fleeing a sinking ship . . .

A SINKING SHIP

91

THIS IS ANOTHER DAY, I KNOW NOT WHAT IT will bring forth, but make me ready, Lord, for whatever it may be. If I am to stand up, help me to stand bravely. If I am to sit still, help me to sit quietly. If I am to lie low, help me to do it patiently. And if I am to do nothing, let me do it gallantly.

GALLANTLY

**A Morning Prayer for Use*
by a Sick Person from
The Book of Common Prayer

92

SHE AND HARRY LIKED TO TRAVEL TO eclipses, the solar ones, they found the lunar ones not so exciting. They would usually arrive at the best location a day or two prior for they enjoyed sunrises too. A particularly memorable sunrise occurred not long before Harry walked on first, the way men do. The sun began coming up but then it stopped. She wasn't certain how long this went on but it was too long she was sure of that. It was a dawn that didn't want to become day. Another unusual thing about that trip was how unfriendly the other campers were, she told me. Just like the people of Bucharest, Harry had said at the time, though as far as I knew they'd never been to, is it, Romania?

COMES A NIGHTMARE

YOU CAN ALWAYS STAY

AWAKE

*Peggy Lee

93

PETER AND DAISY HAD BEEN GOING TO AA meetings for several months and they looked forward to the meetings and wished there were more of them. Then one evening a young man with a horrid beard—everyone had once witnessed a fly staggering out of it—stood up and said to them, "YOU'RE NOT ALCOHOLICS!" He pointed a scrawny accusatory finger at them. This was a first. The others in the room did not want to deal with this one. They chewed at their coffee cups.

"THOSE THAT AIN'T ALCOHOLICS AIN'T!" He hadn't been attending the meetings as long as Peter and Daisy had. "WHATYA COME HERE FOR,

THE COOKIES? MAKE YOUR OWN GODDAMN COOKIES!" His voice was huge.

Daisy wept softly like someone in a courtroom.

"WE HAVE BEEN INFILTRATED BY THESE TWO!" the man screamed.

"We're Peter and Daisy and we're alcoholics," Peter cried.

The others gradually began to align themselves with the bearded man. In retrospect the accuseds' confessions seemed ungenuine.

"Perhaps you've misdiagnosed your problem," someone suggested. They were escorted outside where a mob fell upon them in the street.

THE STREET

94

The older dog's death.

WHAT A PUZZLEMENT THIS

BEING GONE

95

HIS GRANDMOTHER SAID THAT HIS GRAND-father Willing had proposed to her by a skywriting airplane. They were on a beach with hundreds of other people, all strangers. Behind them was a boardwalk with rides and entertainments in progress including a horse who would leap from a high platform into a barrel of water. That day a silver plane flew over it all and wrote *I Love You Aster Marry Me* in letters of smoke.

But the beginning was disappearing even before the end appeared, his grandmother said.

Why did the horse want to jump in a barrel of water? the boy asked.

When no one answered he asked an easier question, What was the horse's name? which they seemed to appreciate.

Mazard, his grandmother replied. She had a little foal who, it was assumed, would take up her duties when she retired from them.

Did you ever see the foal jump into the barrel of water?

No, that boardwalk is long gone now. All those amusements are gone.

Mazard is a good name, he said. Like a magician's name.

It means head, or face, I believe, his grandfather said.

In some other language, the grandmother Aster said, confusing him a little as she often did.

FOAL

96

THE DEVIL HAD A SANDGLASS. ANY MOMENT he would be obliged to invert it. As above, so below. The last shall be first and so on. Time for the flip. Two glass cones connected by their tips—the present instant—now—joining with the past—then—through the most miniscule of apertures. The device was fiendishly simple, invented by a monk, who probably made every effort to count the grains of sand while he was at it. One could only assume he suffered vertiginous headaches and died a madman.

Sometimes the Devil knocked it off its perch—by accident he always told it—but it never broke nor was its process stayed. Indifference to the thing was useless, it could always wait him out. But a time always arrived between aeons when the wretched glass had to be turned and the Devil was the agent of the turning. Each time he resisted but a fog would settle upon him, a sort of trance. This was how the Unmoved Mover worked—the only way He ever got anything done. The Devil regarded the sandglass and felt a migraine approaching. Soon it would begin cartwheeling through his skull. He did not want Azrael to see him so disabled. Curiously, Azrael never noticed the sandglass or if he did, never remarked upon it. Yet he would be the first to succumb to the corresponding void should the Devil fail to reset it. His duties would be eliminated, the manifest of all the souls he carried obliterated. That would make him sad, the Devil thought. And he was already so sad. The Devil could not bear to be the cause of any further dimming of the perfection of his grotesque beauty.

SANDGLASS

97

ARRIVAL

F. Chopin. Op. 28, No.4

98

NOW WHEN THE DEVIL SAW AZRAEL OR, AS IT were, entertained his presence, he worried that he was experiencing the last time he would share his company. This was a recent phenomena and quite unbearable.

Surely there had been a time when the Devil was unaware of him but why try to determine when that was? It had been a time of darkness, puffy yet constricting darkness. There had certainly been nothing to look forward to.

The Devil liked him. He couldn't recall liking anything so much. Such affection could cause nothing but worry of course. The whole apparatus that Azrael embodied, enabled actually, was rickety, not built to last. Deferred maintenance. Delay

delay delay. Judgment stayed forever. Forever and ever. Amen.

Azrael was enlightened but it was through pure ignorance, equipoisal ignorance indistinguishable from depthless wisdom. He had the radiant intelligence of an orphaned octopus larva.

The Devil feared for him. Hadn't he been gone rather longer than usual? Azrael and his duties, his heroic commitment, could drop from God's attention like a stone down a well.

But then he appeared returned once more. Improbable glorious weary sorrowful. Still rejoicing, though the tiniest bit less.

THE ORPHAN

99

Dugong.

DUGONG

JONNO RATTMAN

JOY WILLIAMS is the author of five novels, including *The Quick and the Dead* and most recently *Harrow*, five collections of stories, including *Ninety-Nine Stories of God*, as well as *Ill Nature*, a book of essays that was a finalist for the National Book Critics Circle Award. Among her many honors are the Library of Congress Prize for American Fiction, the Kirkus Prize for Fiction, the *Paris Review*'s Hadada Award, and the Strauss Living Award from the American Academy of Arts and Letters, to which she was elected in 2008. She lives in Arizona and Wyoming.